A long long time ago,
when most people still believed the earth was flat as a pancake,

there lived a king with a beautiful beard ...

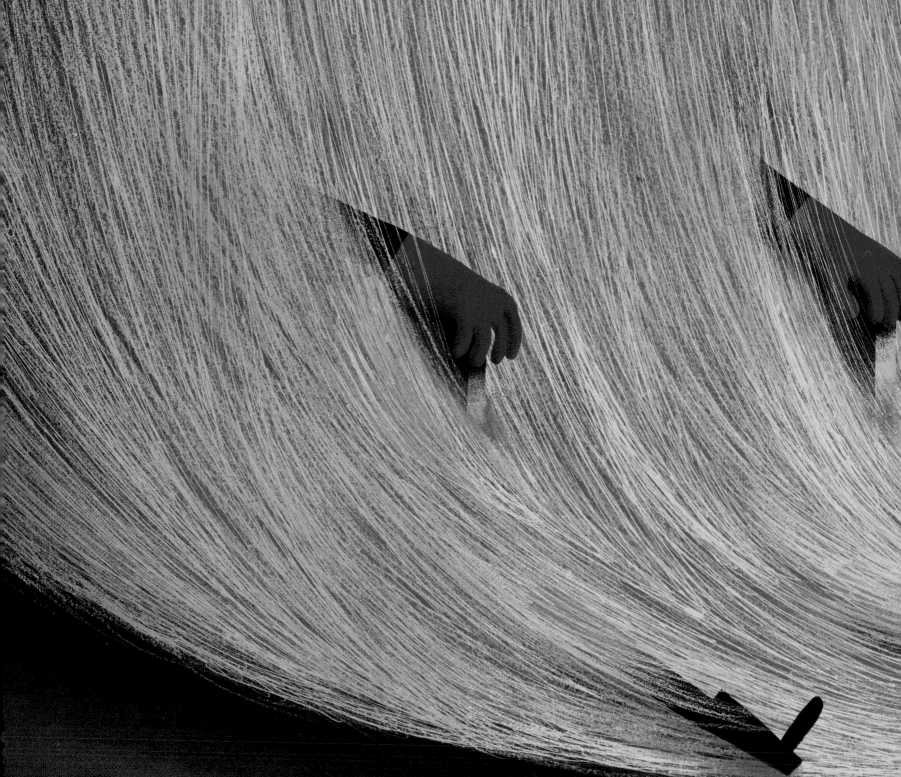

... *shiny as the sun and strong as the wind was*

the King's Golden Beard!

The king loved his kingly self and his beautiful beard so very much that he looked into the mirror every five minutes and thought up special laws to protect his beard and help it grow.

The first law prescribed that the royal beard could never be trimmed.
Another one said that the king alone was allowed to grow a beard.
Even moustaches were outlawed!

So ...

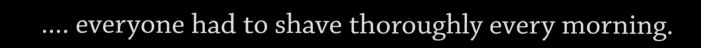

.... everyone had to shave thoroughly every morning.

Whoever dared to break the law and grow one single little hair on his or her face **would be cut into a thousand pieces with a pinchy pair of nail scissors!**

Barbers and bladesmiths flourished. Every chin and cheek in the land was as smooth and soft as butter.

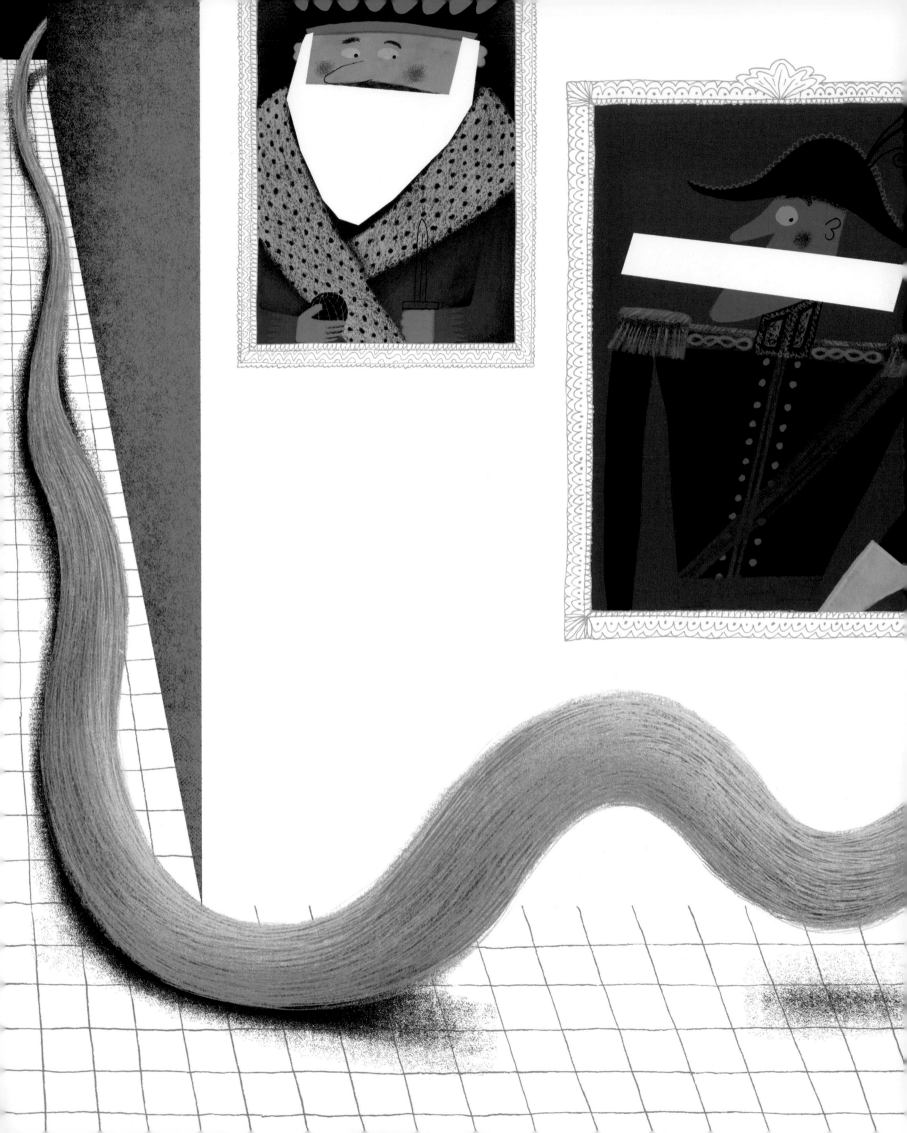

The royal beard kept growing and growing.
It meandered through the vast corridors
of the royal palace ...

.... onto winding garden paths and across **_Royal Beard Street_**. Every single village had one, because that was what another law prescribed.

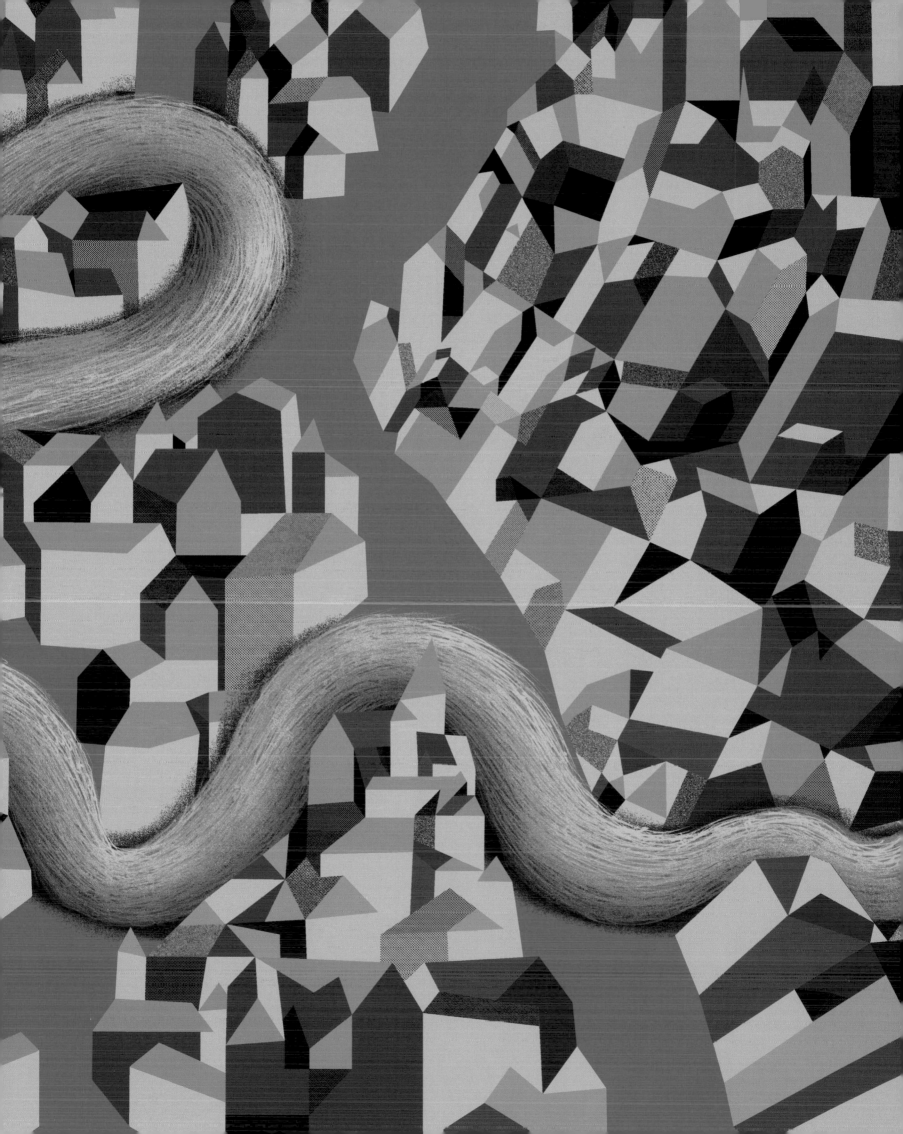

Eventually, the king's golden beard wiggled and waggled its way to the farthest corners of the land. Everyone — man, woman, child, and beast — bowed down to the beard as it swished and swooshed past and disappeared below the horizon.

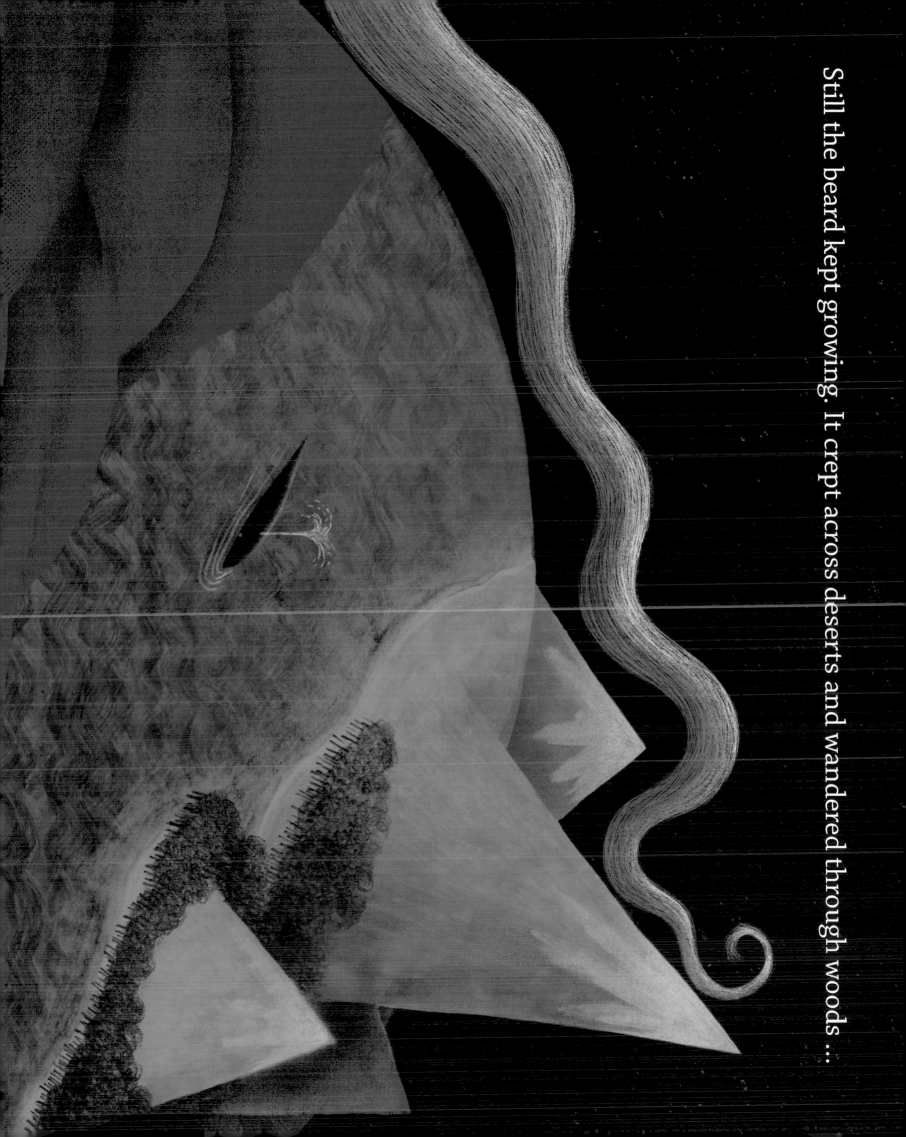

Still the beard kept growing. It crept across deserts and wandered through woods ...

... and sailed over oceans and scaled mountains all around the world.

Finally, the beard rolled up to the back door of the king's palace where it had started its journey long before.

Because the earth, as you know, is round and not flat.

The astronomers, who studied the stars and wrote books about the heavens, had told this to the king, but he scoffed at them.

The king had been sitting on his throne the whole time, barely able to budge as his long, long beard grew longer and longer still.

He was adoring his kingly self in the mirror when **suddenly** a palace guard cried out:

"Strange beard sighted at the back door, sire!"

The king gave the order that the owner of that beard — whoever it was — should be

CUT TO PIECES AT

After all, **the law was the law.**

The royal guards set off to find the culprit ...

... and do as they were told .

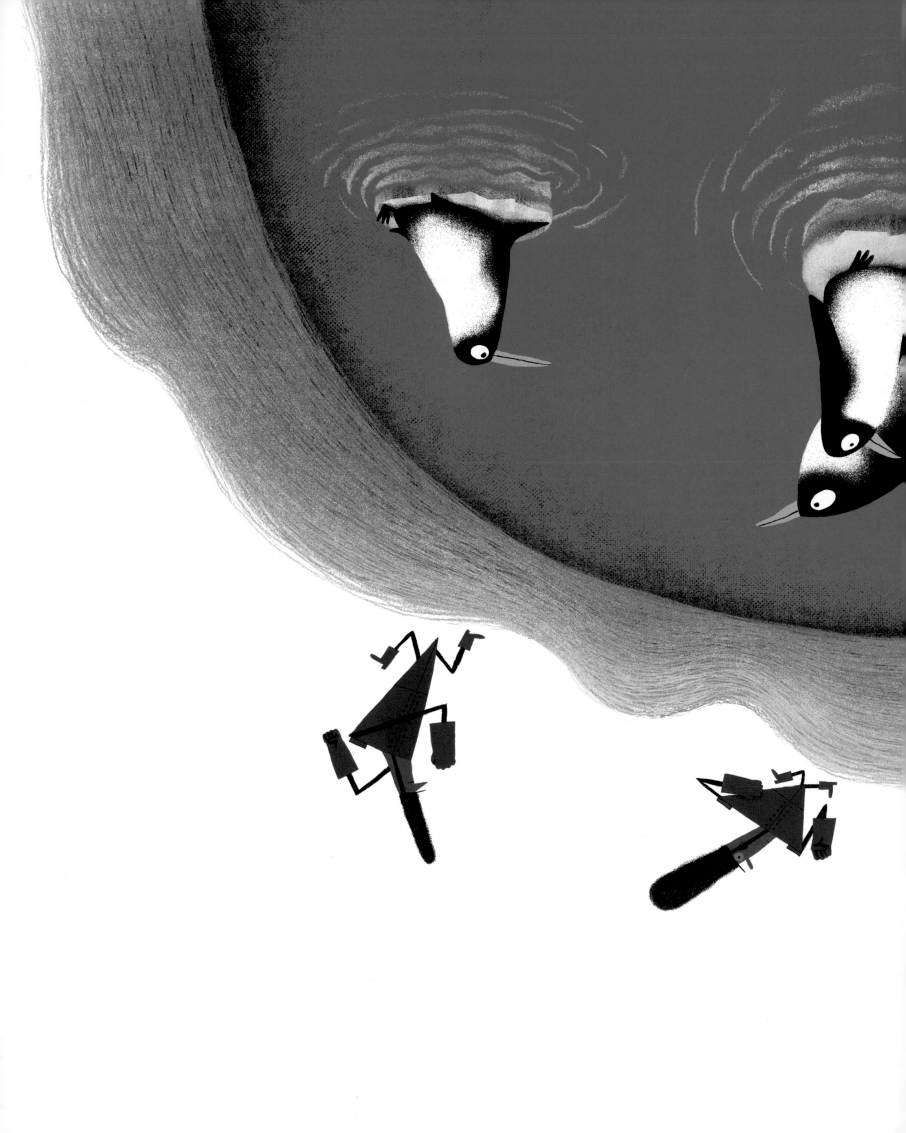

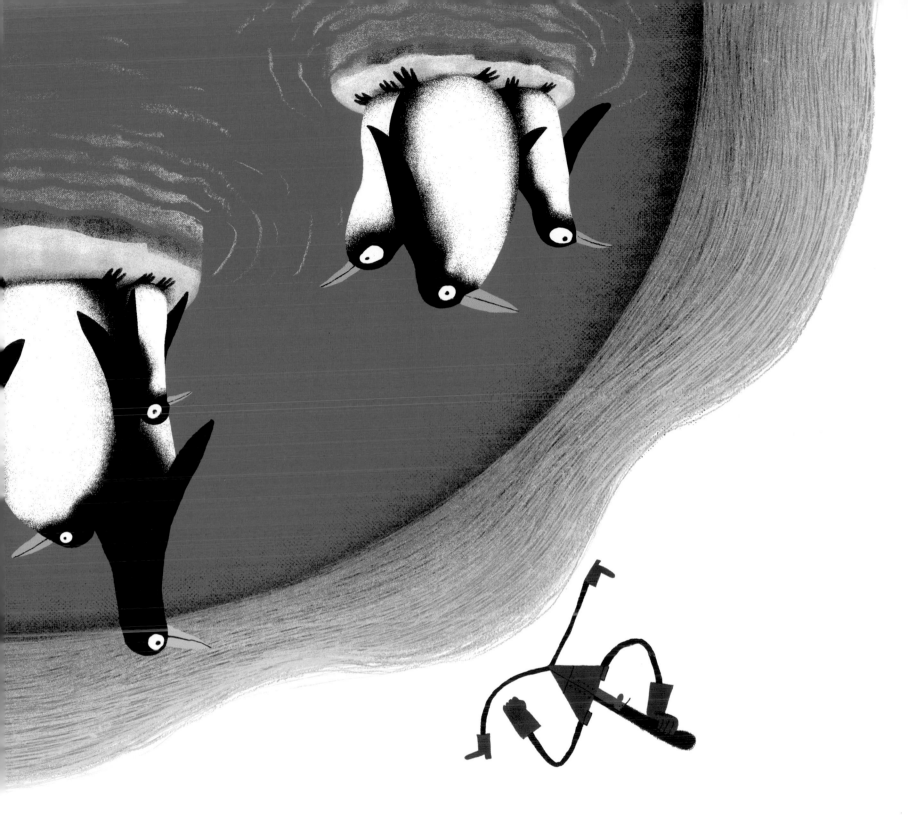

They raced all around the world …

... and arrived at the palace once again.
The king was still sitting on his throne,
still admiring his kingly self in the mirror.

The guards entered and said with one voice:

"Your majesty,
we have found the owner
of the beard."

And so they did.
With a pinchy pair of nail scissors,
because the law is the law.

Shortly after that everyone, kings included, was convinced that the world was as round as an orange.
And the new king was heard to say, "The law may be the law, but *some* laws are very bad for your health."

For my *Golden Petit Soleil*

The King's Golden Beard

Written, illustrated and designed by Klaas Verplancke

North American edition published 2021 by minedition
A Division of Astra Publishing House, New York

Coproduction with Michael Neugebauer Publishing Ltd, Hong Kong
Printed in China in October 2020 at LEO Paper Products Ltd.
Level 9, Telford House, 16 Wang Hoi Road, Kowloon Bay, Hong Kong.
Typesetting in Chaparral Pro

minedition
19 West 21st Street, #1201, New York, NY 10010
e-mail: info@minedition.com
For more information please visit our website: www.minedition.com

Library of Congress Cataloging-in-Publication Data available upon request.

ISBN 978-1-6626-5039-0
First edition
10 9 8 7 6 5 4 3 2 1

a maria russo book
minedition

Klaas Verplancke is supported by Flanders Literature